EVAN *and the* SKYGOATS

EVAN *and the* SKYGOATS

Story by VANESSA VASSAR

Art by OPHELIA CORNET

LeafStormPress
SANTA FE, NEW MEXICO

Evan Delphinus had just turned three when everyone started crying, even the trees. They cried for days and weeks and even months, which were made up of more days and weeks than Evan could count.

Mommy and Poppy took turns holding him when they cried. And when the twigs wept raindrops, Evan hugged the trees, too, because he knew his hugs made everything feel better.

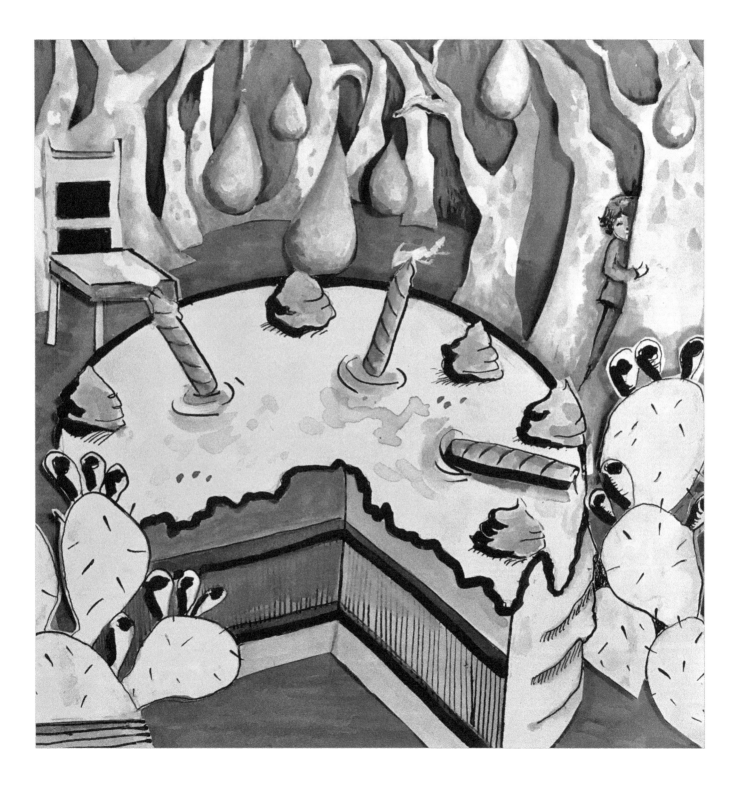

The trees had started weeping when his sister Sky had gotten sick. One day Sky left their home and never came back.

Evan thought that no one so special could completely disappear. He hoped his sister was somewhere high above in the sky. Whenever he went outside, he looked up to the clouds to see if Sky was there.

Most of the time he only saw black crows. They squawked a lot, but Evan didn't know what they were saying.

Mommy said Sky was there in the sky and that they didn't need to see her to feel her.

At times Evan worried that Mommy might float away too. Poppy hugged Evan and told him that Mommy and Poppy were right there with him, and that it was just their thoughts that floated away when they were missing his sister.

Evan understood because sometimes his thoughts did that too.

Often, at nightfall, Poppy took Evan out to see the bats and the moon and the stars.

Evan loved to think of Sky living among all those sparkly stars. He missed her very much and wished she would come back and play music on her cello.

Cello rhymes with yellow. Yellow rhymes with cello.

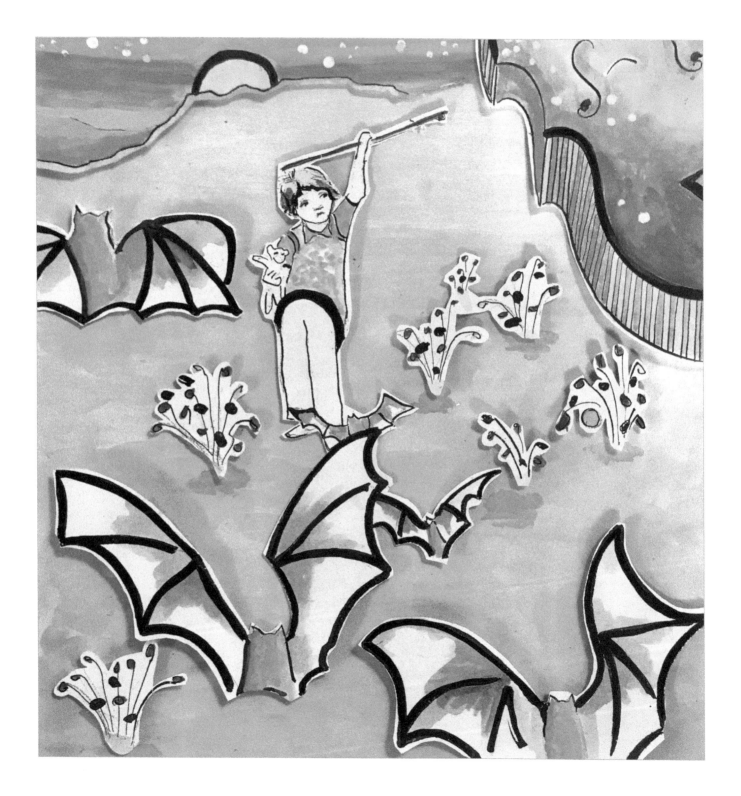

Lots of people came to visit, but Evan liked Camille best of all. He was glad she lived in the house across the plum orchard.

He liked the quiet way Camille walked with him through the gardens and the way she smelled like the spices in his hot apple cider. He especially loved her wild hair.

Evan imagined lights coming out of the tips of her curls like the fireflies he had seen with Sky when they were camping last summer. Sky had pointed to the floating sparkles around them and whispered, "Look, Evan! Fireflies are like little stars."

One day the trees stopped crying. Camille said a warm spring had arrived.

Spring didn't help Mommy stop crying, but she did show Evan some of the colorful new flowers blooming on the farm.

Mommy told him that the blossoms on the fruit trees would soon turn into dark purple plums. Purple was his favorite color, but it was hard for Evan to imagine white blossoms turning into purple plums.

It was on one of these warm spring days that Camille cupped Evan's chin in her hand and smiled. "Ah, *mon petit prince*, I think we need goats."

Camille said the neighbor across the *acequia* had offered them three baby goats. Mommy and Poppy didn't say yes, but they also didn't say no. Evan was so excited that he held his breath and closed his eyes.

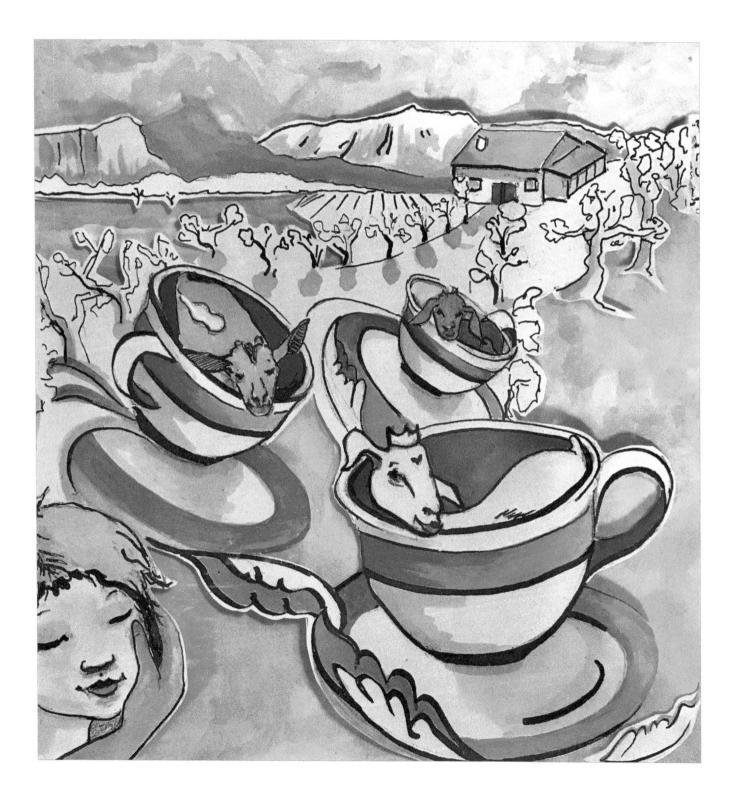

Soon, Poppy began building a little house that he said was a pen for the goats. When he was done, the goats came to live there.

Two of the goats were twins, which Poppy said meant they had been born together at almost the same time from the same mommy and poppy goats.

They named the brown one Evening and the black one Ebony.

The third goat had a marking on her fur that looked like a lightning bolt. Camille asked Evan if he wanted to name her Electra, and he did!

Evan secretly decided that Electra was his twin, even though they had been born on different days. He told her so in a whisper whenever he nuzzled her neck.

Twice a day, Evan went with Camille and Poppy to feed the goats. They drank warm milk from bottles, even though they were almost as big as Evan and he didn't need a bottle anymore.

Eventually, Mommy started visiting the goats too. Once, when Evan was playing with Electra, Mommy laughed out loud like she used to before Sky went away.

Mommy said the goats were sweet and funny like Evan and hugged him without crying.

That evening, Poppy gave Evan a pair of cowboy boots. Poppy said he had worn them as a boy and that Sky had worn them, too.

Poppy's eyelashes were wet, so Evan gave him a big hug before he put them on.

Evan loved the boots and the clatter they made when he ran. He just wished they were goatboy boots instead of cowboy boots. He wanted to have hooves like the goats and climb the way they could!

Evan and Poppy baked bread in the *horno* and climbed up to the treehouse to eat. It was a warm summer night, so Poppy said they could sleep there, too!

He tucked Evan into the crook of his arm and showed him the North Star, explaining how important this star was for travelers.

Evan stared at the North Star for a long time and said he might like to be a traveler.

As the night grew darker and the stars grew brighter, Evan listened while Poppy explained how to connect the stars to draw creatures in the sky.

"The star pictures are called constellations," said Poppy, pointing up. "Look there—Capricornus is a goat with a fish tail."

Evan tried hard to see Capricornus, but he couldn't be sure he was looking at the right stars.

All the stars were pretty.

He listened to Poppy's voice until the words melted into the songs of crickets and frogs and wind and the water in the *acequia*.

And that's when Evan heard someone quietly calling his name. He slipped out of Poppy's arms to see who it was.

Evan rubbed his eyes. "Electra, is that you?"

"Yes, it's me," she whispered.

"I knew you could talk. I knew it!" Evan said.

"Only on starry nights. We goats overheard you saying you'd like to be a traveler. Will you travel into the sky with us tonight?"

Evening and Ebony nodded enthusiastically.

Evan wondered, "Into the sky? But you're goats. You live on land. And don't you sleep at night?"

"We can sleep after exploring. Stars are ever so fun to climb upon," Electra said with a smile.

"But I don't know how. And I'm not a goat," said Evan.

"Well, you're wearing your goatboy boots, so you'll be fine to fly. Just follow us."

The goats stretched their front legs toward the North Star and leaped up into the sky.

Evan looked down at his feet and saw that his boots had turned into goat hooves. Soon, he was climbing, too, just like the goats!

Magical creatures of every shape and size greeted them as they stepped through the stars.

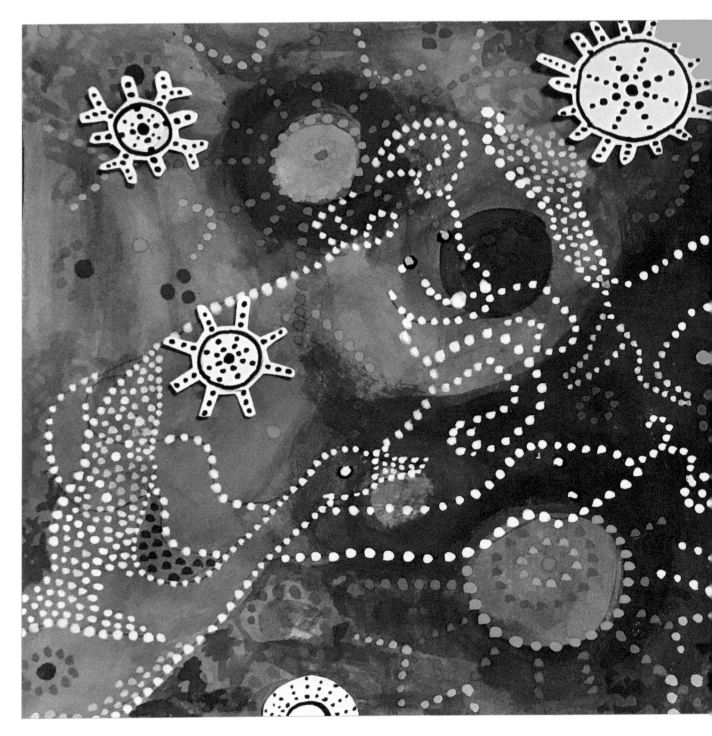

They met Cygnus the swan, Taurus the bull, Pavo the peacock, Hydra the sea

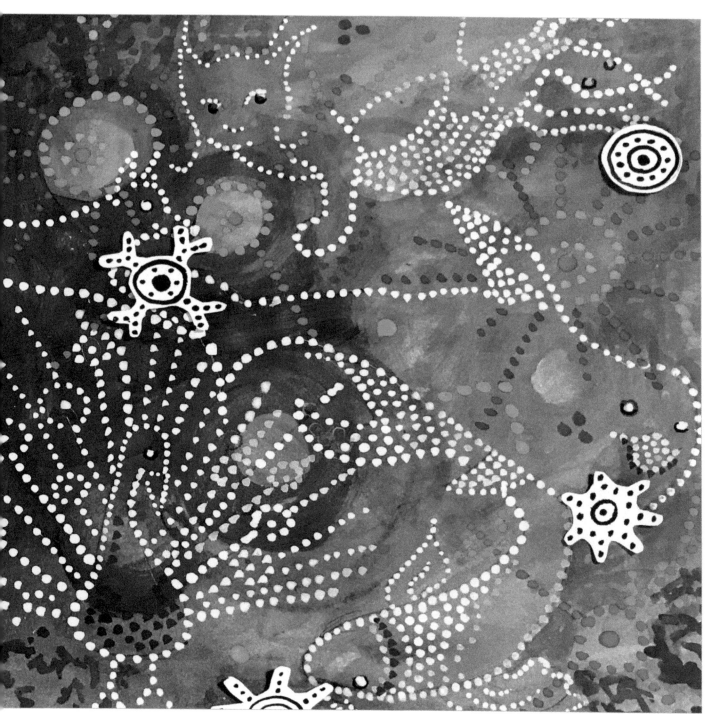

serpent, a lynx, a lizard, a flying fish, a fox, and even Delphinus the dolphin!

Electra pointed to a group of stars ahead, and Evan watched as the constellation turned into a goat with a fish tail. It was Capricornus! His horns adorned him like the crown of a wise king, and his tail sparkled.

"Greetings, little one," he said warmly.

"Hello," Evan replied, looking at him curiously. "If you are a goat, why do you have a fish tail?"

"Hmmm," Capricornus said, with a twinkle in his eye. "I should ask, if you are a boy, why do you have goat hooves?"

"Well, to climb through the stars, of course!" said Evan.

"Well, I needed to swim through a river once long ago," Capricornus explained.

"We are all constantly changing," Capricornus said, smiling at Evan and the Skygoats. "Sometimes even our biggest changes are invisible to others."

And with a slight bow and swish of his fish tail, Capricornus waved them onward.

Evan's eyes began to feel heavy. He turned to Electra, Evening, and Ebony as a gentle wind caught them and carried them dreamily downward.

The farm soon came into view, and Evan could see the *acequia* shimmering in the light of the moon.

He waved a sleepy goodnight to his traveling companions as they parted ways.

Evan had already settled back into the tree house bed when he realized that he hadn't seen his sister Sky during his travels.

Was she there in the sky? How could he know? Evan stared at the stars intently. He drew a line with his finger connecting the brightest stars above him and found he had drawn a cello.

Sky was there! She really was!

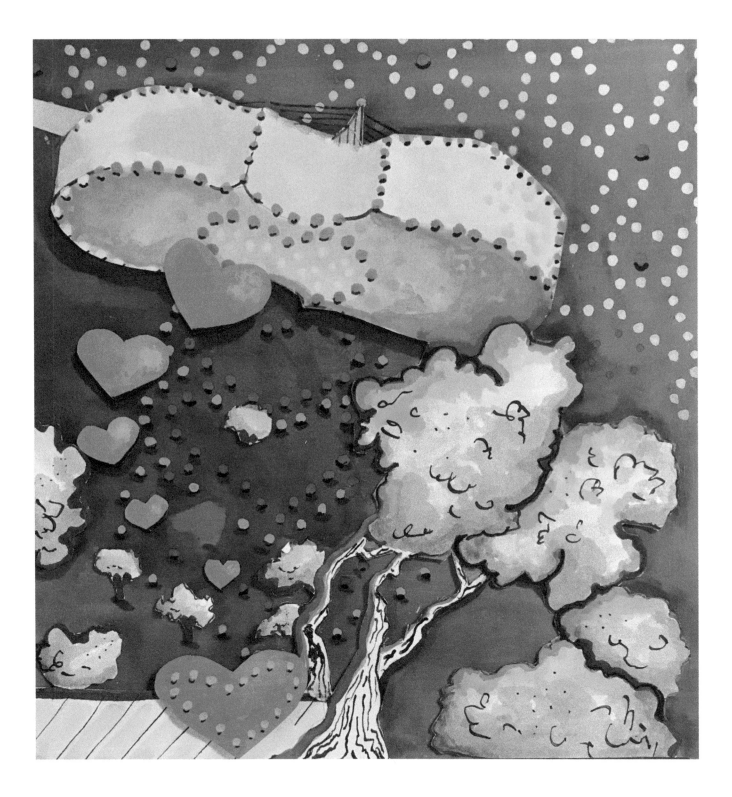

Evan sighed happily and snuggled in next to Poppy. As he did, he realized that Mommy's arm was around him too. Maybe she had climbed up into the tree house to be closer to Sky just like he had.

Evan smiled. And as his eyes closed, he swirled and twirled into a sweet and sparkling sleep.

●　●　●

This book is dedicated to the memory of
Sky Velvet Vassar (1996–2010),
whose grace and wisdom far surpassed
the thirteen years of her life.

And to all the young people who are
forever and always so dearly missed.

About the Author

VANESSA VASSAR grew up in California and received degrees in communication arts and English. She traveled extensively with her work and lived in New York and Berlin before settling in New Mexico. Her love of storytelling has been the basis of her professional work in journalism, film, music, and photography. Vanessa was inspired to write *Evan and the Skygoats* after the passing of her daughter, Sky Velvet. In the free fall of grief, Vanessa found her first glimmer of hope visiting a local goat farm. She fell in love with the gentle and playful nature of the goats and eventually brought three baby goats home. Vanessa lives with her family in Albuquerque.

About the Illustrator

OPHELIA CORNET was born in Belgium to a family of artists and designers. Her life in the Belgian countryside was juxtaposed with annual visits to New York City, where influential artists were among her family friends. Ophelia went on to study painting and photography, and her current work includes oil paintings, tile murals, and sculpture. She has been the Lead Art Instructor at the Albuquerque Museum for nineteen years. Ophelia lives with her family in an old adobe house in New Mexico and enjoys traveling to the South of France, Guatemala, and Mexico. Ophelia loved and admired Sky.

Ophelia and Vanessa met through their daughters, Sofia and Sky, who shared a beautiful friendship.

VanessaVassar.com   OpheliaCornet.com

LOVE THOUGHTS FOR SOMEONE GRIEVING

1. Be gentle with yourself.

2. Listen to yourself to know what is best for your personal healing.

3. Find healing places in nature and spend time in them often—like leaning into a tree or taking in the stars of a night sky.

4. Perform small rituals that connect you with who or what you most miss. Plant a tree, gather flowers, collect heart rocks, build stone sculptures, draw your loved one's name in the sand, light a candle, burn sage, create an altar, send biodegradable balloons off into the sky, blast music in the car. Trust yourself to know what works for you.

5. Be willing to pause a friendship. Understand that some people, despite their best intentions, will not know how to hold space for your grief and may even avoid the subject of your loss. Focus on spending time with those from your past who help you the most in the present.

6. Be open to allowing new friends into your life who are able to be with who you are now.

7. Communicate with those who have lived through a similar loss. Grief support groups or professional counselors may be helpful to you. Be open to trying this again with different people at different stages of your grief.

8. Spend time with pets and farm animals that feel comforting to you. Slow down to watch other creatures on our planet earth. Observe a colony of bats, listen to an orchestra of crickets, or follow a single firefly at night.

9. Accept that grief comes in waves and that each wave is different. Some will crash into you with extreme anger, others will roll softly through you with profound sadness. Grief can also bring with it exhaustion, guilt, numbness, denial, hyperactivity. Give yourself permission to step out of the waves of grief whenever you are able, even with mindless distractions.

10. Forgive yourself whenever possible for whatever you possibly can.

11. Be in the present as often as you are able to be, allowing for the unchanging past and the unpredictable future.

12. Accept that the only constant in the world is change.

LOVE THOUGHTS FOR THOSE SUPPORTING SOMEONE GRIEVING

1. Be gentle with anyone grieving.
2. Sit with someone grieving quietly and consistently. Allow them to be comforted by your presence without your own demands or agendas.
3. Listen thoughtfully to someone grieving without expecting immediate outcomes.
4. Refrain from making sweeping statements like:

   > *Everything happens for a reason.*

   Or putting yourself first:

   > *I don't know what I would do if I was you.*
   >
   > *I can't imagine what you're going through.*
   >
   > *I could never be as strong as you.*

   Don't compare your own life:

   > *When I heard your child passed away, I hugged mine even tighter.*

   Or pronounce what you think is best:

   > *Getting back to school/work/sports/friend activities will cheer you up!*

   Instead, ask with specificity:

   > *Would you like to have a walk with me by the river/mountain/ocean/ park? Can I take you to/bring you lunch today? Can I pick up anything from the store for you? Can I give you a ride anywhere?*

5. Rather than using a generic statement like:

   > *I'm so sorry for your loss.*

   Speak from your heart:

   > *I love you.*
   >
   > *I'm thinking of you.*
   >
   > *I loved it when your daughter/son/sibling . . .*

6. If you don't know the grieving person or the person who passed very well (or at all), perform small acts of kindness:

    I brought you a cup of coffee/water/tea, a candle, flowers, a meal, a heart-shaped rock, a healing stone, a pomegranate, an apple, a book, a game, a stuffed animal . . .

7. Be mindful that a grieving person's faith, religion or spiritual beliefs may be different from your own.

8. Understand that small children grieve differently than older children and adults do. A small child will often worry about the present situation and may not grasp that death is final. A slightly older child may worry about his or her own health, whereas a teenager may have thoughts of guilt and self-blame. Check in to understand how you or someone else can help alleviate this stress.

9. Ask yourself if you are trying to urge a grieving person to put his or her grief away and move on too soon because you are uncomfortable. Time in and of itself does not heal all wounds.

10. Shock takes on many forms and identities in order to protect the person grieving. Don't assume a grieving person is fine if they are functioning.

11. If a young person has passed away, focus on the meaning rather than the length of life.

12. Accept that the only constant in the world is change.

●   ●   ●

PUBLISHED BY
Leaf Storm Press
Post Office Box 4670
Santa Fe, New Mexico 87502
USA
leafstormpress.com

Leaf Storm Press titles are available at bulk discounts for special events and premiums..
For more information please contact the publisher at leafstormpress@gmail.com.

Book design by LSP Graphics
Design & Editorial Consultant: Sofia Resnik

First edition.
Printed in the US

10 9 8 7 6 5 4 3 2

Library of Congress Control Number: 2019940900
Cataloging-in-Publication Data is on file.

ISBN 978-1-9456520-4-2

CPSIA information can be obtained
at www.ICGtesting.com
Printed in the USA
LVHW070335210919
631750LV00001B/3/P